Hope in the Storm

Written by Christi Thompson

Illustrated by Janet Cornett

He made the storm be still, and
the waves of the sea were hushed.
~Psalm 107:29~

Copyright © 2020 by Christi Thompson

All rights reserved. This book or any portion thereof may not be reproduced, used, or transmitted in any form or by any means whatsoever, electronic or mechanical, including photocopying, recording, or any information storage and retrieval system, without the express written permission from Christi Thompson except for the use of brief quotations in a book review. Your support of the author's rights is appreciated.

ISBN 9-7817069449-9-7

While some parts of this book were inspired by first hand accounts of real events, the characters are fictitious. Any similarity to real persons, living or dead, is coincidental and not intended by the author.

Printed and bound in the United States of America
Second Printing, 2020

Visit the author's website at www.youareabeautifulcreation.com

As we seek to help children make sense of adversity the most important thing we can do is to provide safety, stability, and attuned love.

"We are fearfully and wonderfully made."
~Psalm 139~

The story we tell about our experiences is known as our narrative. The structure of this book is purposeful and provides an example of a complete healthy narrative, including the beginning, middle, and end of Hope's experience. The placement of positive resources before and after the adverse events in this story are intentional. It highlights what we know from trauma research will be integral to the healing process. All the positive support and resources surrounding the adverse experience will naturally help facilitate the integration process in the brain of the separated parts becoming whole.

In the back of this book you will find more information About This Book as well as resource worksheets. You are welcome to make copies of these worksheets. They are also available for download through the author's website at www.youareabeautifulcreation.com. We only ask that you credit the author's work.

Helpful Hints

This is a "together" book, meant to be read with a trusted adult. As we grow and learn, two brains are better than one and Jesus gives us these relationships to support our development.

DO read this in parts if your little one has a shorter attention span or is younger. This book is separated intentionally for that purpose.

DON'T read "The Scary Thing" by itself. (This is the only part of the book that I recommend you definitely sandwich between the resourcing parts that come before and after it.) Remember we need those positive resources on both sides of the story.

DO be attuned and available to listen, love, and clarify as your child processes. You are the expert and are attuned to helping your child notice and develop their own resources.

DON'T push your child to share details about a traumatic experience, as it may be harmful. Naming the experience with one or two words is different than describing the details of an experience. Details can re-traumatize.

DO use the worksheets that have been provided at the back to gently guide your child as they identify their resources, name their experience, and begin tell their story.

"Do not be afraid of sudden terror or of the ruin of the wicked, when it comes, for the LORD will be your confidence and will keep your foot from being caught."

Proverbs 3:25-26

This Book is lovingly Dedicated to each and every person impacted by
Hurricane Michael on October 10, 2018
may you always find Hope
and also to
Ella, Olivia, Emma and Spencer
&
Mrs. Arlene Stevens

I am forever grateful that Jesus decided we should meet
and for the inspiring faith of Mrs. Dartha Ellis.

Part 1

Hello Friends . . . . … 1

The Scary Thing 5

During the Storm 7

After the Storm 13

Part 2

Grammy Explains How God Made Me 17

Grammy Helps Me Think About Thinking 21

Hidden Treasure 31

Part 1

HELLO FRIENDS

Hi, I'm Hope... I live on the Forgotten Coast in Florida with my family. Mom and Dad say we are lucky because our whole family lives here--grandparents, aunts, uncles, and cousins.

It's a lot of fun at my grandparent's house after church on Sundays!!

Our house is close to the beach. There are so many wonderful things about living just down the street and around the corner from the beach!! We love spending the day playing in the ocean, building sandcastles, and discovering amazing sea creatures.

Mom thinks we have the most beautiful sunsets in the whole wide world. I think so too!! Sometimes we get to stay on the beach after the sun goes down and build a bonfire.

I love it when our whole family comes and we get to stay up past our bedtime, look for ghost crabs, and lie on a blanket under the stars. Grammy sits on her favorite quilt and points out the stars. "God knows each one by name," she says, "and He knows your name too. The same God who made the stars holds you, and you, and me," she tells us.

My Grammy loves spending time at the beach with all of us, and she loves Jesus. She loves Jesus a whole lot and she trusts Him too, even when things are terribly scary.

THE SCARY THING

Last fall on October 10th, we had a storm so big it was called a Hurricane. It was super-duper scary, terrifying actually!

The WIND and the RAIN are BIG in a Hurricane. Too much wind and too much rain, **SO** much wind and **SO** much rain that it caused damage and flooding.

Some things got washed away like cars, and toys, and clothes, and couches and even pieces of houses, some whole houses too. This was not the good kind of washing--like when we get dirty and have to wash off in the bathtub. It made everything even dirtier, so maybe it was more like sloshing than washing.

Trees blew down, and roofs were torn off. My church kind of got knocked down, all the insides got sloshed around, and even my school was banged up. It was NOT fun!

There was no power for a long time and TOO much damage. After the storm, there were scary noises like alarms; some kids said this was the scariest part, but I thought the scariest part was during the storm.

DURING THE STORM

My family stayed together at my grandparents' house during the storm. My parents and grandparents had been through storms before, but no one expected the force of this storm. In the middle of the storm, the water began trickling under the door. Mom and Dad were working to scoop it out and find the safest place for us in the house. I did not like the noises--they were terribly scary, terrifying actually.

Mom asked me to go to my grandma's room--I figured that she would be having a talk with Jesus about this storm. But do you know how I found her? She was asleep in her chair!! I am not kidding! There was Grammy taking a nap in the middle of the hurricane. I ran over and shook her knees, "Grammy, how can you take a nap at a time like this?? Don't you realize we are in the middle of a hurricane?!?!?"

Grammy heard the panic in my voice and saw the fear in my eyes. She cupped my face in her hands and gently reminded me, "Baby girl, Jesus slept in the storm." Pulling me into her lap, she began to tell me the story I had heard so many times before. . .

"Now Jesus was on the boat with his disciples. It had been a long day, and Jesus was resting his eyes when a storm began to blow. The wind was howling and they were being tossed on the waves. The disciples were in fear for their lives, and Jesus was taking a nap. 'Wake up!' they said, 'Don't you care that we're all about to die!' Of course He cared, but He wasn't worried. He simply stated, 'Peace, Be Still,' and the winds and the waves obeyed."

"Grammy," I said, "I sure do wish Jesus was here right now so He could talk some sense into this storm." Grammy smiled warmly and a spirit of peace radiated from her eyes as she told me, "I think He'll be back soon enough and you can rest assured, His Holy Spirit is here with us even now child."

"Grammy, I wish this storm and these scary noises would stop. I don't like them one little bit. It sounds like the whole earth is groaning."

Grammy smiled again, "My dear child, I think you are right. Romans 8:22 tells us that God's creation will groan in pain. Sounds like an accurate description of what we are hearing, don't you think so, Hope?"

I did think so, and I thought it sounded like the earth must be in a whole lot of pain because it groaned and moaned and howled! I was worried and scared, terrified actually. "Grammy, what should we do?" I asked.

Grammy responded with confidence, "Baby girl, the Bible helps us there, too. You see, we know Jesus will always help in times of trouble."

"If you keep on reading right there in Romans it says we must be patient and have Hope," she winked, giving me a squeeze. "The storm will pass and God will help us rebuild in time until one day when He will come to restore His whole creation."

"While we wait, let's sing a bit. Bring me my hymnal will you?" So I took a deep breath and slid off Grammy's lap. Everyone else had begun to gather in her room; Dad held me tight, and Grammy started to sing as I handed her the book. When people ask me how long the storm lasted, I tell them: "through one nap, a couple of Bible stories, and almost every song in Grammy's big red songbook!"

AFTER THE STORM

Grammy was right! The storm passed by. The wind and the rain stopped. Then came the saddest part of the storm because we saw all the damage, but we didn't just see it--we felt it too. We felt sad and mad, helpless and confused, then mad and sad some more.

It was hard to see all the people and places we loved in such bad shape. Lots and lots of places we loved were gone or badly damaged--our church, our favorite restaurant, our friends' houses. Some people had nowhere to live and all of their clothes, and furniture, and even their toys were gone.

Our house was damaged too--we could still live there, but it needed A LOT of work. This was the boring part because everyone was so busy that they didn't have as much time to play.

"Sad and mad and bored!" I stomped a few weeks after the storm. "I'm sorry mommy, I just am!" "I see. I guess it feels like there's no time for Hope?" Mom responded. "If there's one thing we definitely need, it's time for Hope! Let's make a play plan, a special time every day for us to connect and play. It will be good for all of us!" And, mom was right! Somehow knowing that no matter what our day held we would have our special time made the hardest days feel easier.

My best friend had to move to Georgia; I cried. Mom and Dad held me close and said it was okay to feel sad. They also felt sad, but better days were ahead. They said they felt all of those same feelings too, even scared, terrified actually. Just like Grammy, Mom and Dad love Jesus a whole lot and they trust Him to help in times of trouble.

Part 2

GRAMMY EXPLAINS HOW GOD MADE ME
(and my Feelings)

One day Mom and Grammy took me to the beach to take a break from all the work and have some fun. Our day was going great! We were building sandcastles and jumping waves, but then I looked up and saw some dark clouds headed our way. All of a sudden, I was filled with panic and I wanted to run away, far away, because I was terrified actually!

I ran to Mom and Grammy and screamed, "We need to leave now! The Hurricane is coming back! Let's get in the car and drive straight to Georgia, actually let's head for Tennessee-- NOW!!!"

Mom looked up at the sky a little concerned, "We probably do need to start packing up soon, but I don't think we need to drive all the way to Georgia, Hope. What do you think Grammy?"

Mom placed me in Grammy's lap and as she looked into my eyes with love she said, "Baby girl, just because it feels like the hurricane is coming back, doesn't mean that it is. Why don't you help me put our toys in the bag and then sit with me on the blanket for a moment while Mom loads the wagon? When we get home, I want to share something very special about how God made you and me, but for now let's sing,"--and she began to sing our special song as she cuddled me close.

Later, when we were back at Grammy's house, she pulled me into her lap. "I want you to understand that what happened on the beach today was just part of how God made you and me--all of his children actually."

"You see, we have a very special part of our brain that God designed to help protect us in times of danger or trouble. We can call it the 'A-team' and when the A-team receives the call that we might be in trouble the only choices it gives is to run away, or fight, or freeze in fear, or flat out faint."

"It can keep us safe, but sometimes it tries to help us when we don't actually need help. That's what happened today. Seeing those dark clouds, hearing the thunder, and feeling the wind pick up made you remember the storm and signaled your A-team that you might be in danger, so you wanted to run away from the danger."

"I know you weren't thinking about the BIG storm, but the A-team gets a call from one or more of our five senses. You know about those right, Hope?"

GRAMMY HELPS ME THINK ABOUT THINKING (and my Feelings)

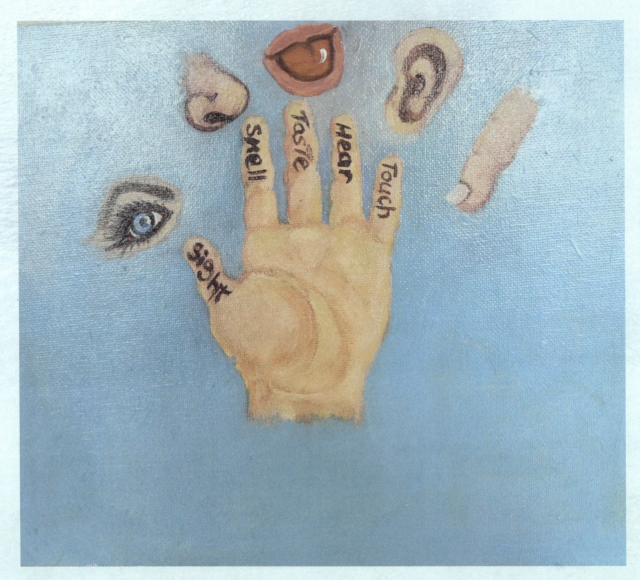

"Yes, seeing, hearing, smelling, tasting, and touching! I love my five senses! We've talked about them in school. We even came up with a list of all the things we love about each of them!" I remembered. "That's wonderful, how fun!" Grammy smiled. "Well, that's who called the A-team up inside your brain."

"You see, Hope, we hold inside of us all of our memories and experiences," Grammy continued, "And if you think about it, I bet what you felt today on the beach was very much like what you felt during the storm, wasn't it?"

I tried to think about what Grammy was saying. I really just wanted to run off that beach as fast as I could.

"Well, yes, I guess SO. I was terrified actually." Now I was feeling silly for wanting to go all the way to Georgia, well actually Tennessee, and a little bit ashamed for screaming at Mom and Grammy. "I am sorry, Grammy. I feel embarrassed," I admitted.

"Well Hope, you have nothing to apologize for my sweet baby girl. That's why I am telling you all of this so that you understand that you are wonderfully made and the A-team is just trying to help. Mom and I knew it was just a regular old afternoon thunderstorm that was still pretty far away and we were all perfectly safe, but you didn't feel safe. The reason you felt like we were in danger and your feelings were so BIG is because they were memories from the BIG storm--memories from your 5 senses. You were designed this way for a reason, to protect you from danger, and today you felt like there was danger," Grammy explained.

"Hope, Where does our help come from?"

"That's easy Grammy! From the man upstairs!!! Psalm 121, He's the maker of Heaven and Earth," I exclaimed.

"That's right Hope, and He is also the maker of you and I. Think about all the houses that are being re-built right now. Have you noticed which floor the builders construct first, and what comes next?"

"The bottom floor is first, then the top floor, Silly!!" I giggled thinking about trying to build the top floor first.

"Well, that's also how God designed your brain, Hope, and the top floor is the part we are using right now to think about our thoughts and our feelings and just by doing that it helps us calm down."

"Your top floor is still under construction and adults get to help you build it. As a matter of fact we are doing that right now!" Grammy lovingly explained.

"Once you understand how you are designed, you can begin to think about using the Top Floor of your brain to make choices about what to do when the A-team is called up-- listening to Grammy sing or hugs or drawing pictures will send the all-clear message back using your 5 senses. Don't forget to tell the A-team thank you for trying to be helpful." Grammy reminded me with a smile.

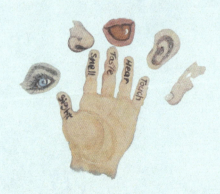

"I don't want you to think the A-team is bad; it is just sometimes way too eager to help, Grammy continued,

'Thanks, but no thanks! I don't think I need to go all the way to Tennessee today, and I DO have other choices; not just A-team choices, but thank you for trying to keep me safe.'

It's okay to feel BIG feelings. It was a BIG storm that we went through, wasn't it. . . but guess who's BIGGER?"

"I know, Grammy, God is bigger; He's the biggest and so is His love. I guess I did start to feel better after we started singing, but I was still a little scared," I confided.

"Of course you were Hope. It's okay to feel scared, even terrified. Our feelings give us information. When we calm down and understand them, we can use God's word to help us make wise choices."

"You know, the first time after the hurricane that I saw a storm in the distance on one of my beach walks, I felt scared too. But as I took in His Beautiful Creation all around me, I prayed and asked for God's help and I finished my walk feeling peaceful and secure."

"God designed our brains to help keep us safe. His plan is for us to grow stronger from the hard times and we can do that when we place our trust in Him. The Bible teaches us to bring all our worries and concerns to God and to take our thoughts captive to obey Christ. He teaches us how to see our story through His eyes."

"Do you remember what Jesus said to the storm and how the storm obeyed?" Grammy asked.

"Yes, Grammy, I remember. 'Peace, be still.' I was wishing he would talk some sense into that hurricane." I thought about how loud the storm had been.

"Oh, Oh, I see!!!!" I exclaimed. "I can use what He said on the A-team, right? I know what Jesus would say to the A-team, 'Peace, be still.' You know it is kind of like having a storm inside of you. . . All those BIG feelings? Peace, be still--yep, now I'm ready to use my 5 senses to send the all-clear message to the A-team. You know WE are HIS creation TOO, after all."

"Hope, you are absolutely right, and you most certainly are a beautiful creation of our loving, all-knowing, all powerful God. I know He has wonderful plans for you my sweet child."

HIDDEN TREASURE

One good thing about our hurricane, was that we learned A LOT. Mom said that even though we knew Hurricane Michael was coming, the grown-ups didn't have all of the information because they didn't know what questions to ask. Now, the grown-ups know what questions to ask, and then they will know how to keep everyone super-duper safe, so I don't have to worry about hurricanes anymore.

And, I learned that I can always trust God's truth and look to Him for guidance. He has given me a wonderful family to help me grow and learn and I can trust them to keep me safe. They love me so so much and I love them too!!! I learned that it's okay to feel our feelings and we should never be ashamed of our feelings because they are part of how God made us. We should love each and every part of ourselves (like the A-team) and ask for Jesus to help us every. single. day.

We Love Jesus and he loves us and we can trust in Him to show us the way. My Grammy was right about so many things. She was right about how God would help us to rebuild and about God's plans for me. Our school was repaired and classes began again.

Last week Grammy had a special surprise for me, a treasure hunt-- I love treasure hunts! At first, I was worried when it started to rain, but then Grammy started dancing. We danced and played and jumped in puddles, it was SO MUCH FUN!!!! Grammy says that God has given us hidden treasure and our play date in the rain was treasure!

I have been finding treasures everywhere!! The green grass growing and the flowers blooming are some of my favorite treasure. I love to play with my friends and we have even met some new friends that just moved to town--new treasures. My church meets at our elementary school for now, and this has been cool for so many reasons. We are going to build a new church, but we discovered something wonderful . . .

Our church wasn't a building, it is the people, ALL the people (from so many different places), so whether we are at school, on the beach, or in a tent—WE are the church! Talk about discovering hidden treasure!!! There have been so many amazing people that God has sent to help us along the way and I treasure each one of them——Teachers, counselors, workers (with some pretty cool equipment), even singers, and we have had a bunch of parties and BBQs with all of our new friends.

I think seeing how much people love us and love Jesus is one of the most precious treasures. Of course, I do have a super duper favorite out of all of these things. And I have to tell you that I think God sent it JUST FOR US as a reminder to look for TREASURE in unexpected places--Would you believe there is a sunflower growing on top of our school?? TRUE STORY!! Talk about finding treasure, WOW!!! It gives us HOPE for all of the wonderful things that God has in store for us and reminds us that he will bring treasures out of our darkest times--that is His specialty after all!!!

The Story Behind the Story

I stand in awe of our God and how He truly goes before and behind us working all things for good for His namesake. In May of 2018, many months before Hurricane Michael and hundreds of miles away from Mexico Beach, I spoke in our community in North Georgia about Trauma Awareness. The event entitled "Hope in the Storm" was meant to reference the figurative storms we face in life.

About five months later I spent a week at St. Joe Beach with my boys and my husband on fall break. As they played on the beach, and I prepared to lead a women's conference, God continued to lay the groundwork in my heart. Ten days after we left, the Mexico Beach/Port St. Joe community was hit with the devastating force of Hurricane Michael. The destruction and trauma this precious community had endured was hard to fathom. We prayed.

During the weeks that followed, we continued to be constant in prayer. Then one day, while I was praying for a particular woman (I had never met), the Holy Spirit whispered to call her and let her know we were praying. "But I don't know her," was my first response, "Call her," came the command. Our ministry team had coined the phrase, "Yes sir, Daddy." How else could I respond? I guess you could say the rest is history.

God provided the opportunity to serve His people--witnessing His faithfulness was humbling. Along the way, I heard inspiring stories and saw evidence of His love and power at work in the lives of His children, young and old. The inspiration for this book was born.

Many pieces of the story are based on real-life events. A wise Christ-centered woman took a nap in the middle of the hurricane in Lynn Haven, FL and when her panicked daughter rushed to wake her, she replied, "Baby girl, Don't you know Jesus slept in the storm." The daughter recounted this testimony to a stranger in a coffee shop (me), recalling how at those words she was flooded with a peace that passes understanding, as the earth groaned. Churches, homes, and lives were lost, yet in the midst people saw God's faithfulness. A sunflower grew on top of Port St. Joe Elementary School and children, young and old, rejoiced.

Hurricane Michael made landfall in Mexico Beach, Florida on October 10, 2018 as a Category 5. It was the strongest hurricane on record to hit the Florida panhandle. In terms of pressure, it was the third strongest in recorded history, behind the 1935 Labor Day hurricane and Hurricane Camille of 1969. Wind speeds of 160 mph ranked it as the fourth strongest hurricane ever to make landfall in the contiguous United States. Hurricane Michael left an unimaginable path of destruction in its wake, leaving the communities that it impacted forever changed. Recovery will continue for years to come. Our thoughts and prayers continue to be with these communities.

This photo of my boys was taken on September 23, 2018 and has become a reminder for us that our God is faithful and to have Hope in the Storm.

About the Author

Christi Thompson lives with her husband Scott and their two adventurous boys in North Georgia. They love to camp, explore wildlife, and spend time in God's incredible creation.

She is a licensed professional counselor, who is passionate about helping the community and her clients understand that we are designed to heal from trauma.

In 2017, answering a call to ministry, she founded Beautiful Creation, a community outreach ministry. The mission statement, "Live in Joy, Nuture Hope," speaks to the belief about life after healing from trauma.

Beautiful Creation events and sponsors help fund the "Hope in the Storm Campaign," which provides trauma counseling scholarships and services to those impacted by trauma. Christi has served churches, storm victims, ministry leaders, and other individuals in need through the "Hope in the Storm Campaign."

Together, we can make a difference in the lives of people who have experienced trauma. Beautiful Creation would love to partner with your church or organization!

Connect with Christi on Instagram and Facebook
@you.are.a.beautiful.creation
www.facebook.com/abeautifulcreation

Visit www.youareabeautifulcreation.com
to schedule a book reading or for more information
about supporting the "Hope in the Storm Campaign."

About the Illustrator

Janet Cornett has painted since she was seven years old. She grew up in Decatur, and moved to Gainesville 26 years ago. She really became serious about painting in 1999.

She paints every day and paints mainly commissions for other people. Oil is her medium and still-life her favorite subject. Family is most important to her and her passion for painting.

She embraced the opportunity to illustrate this book, which she felt offers a hopeful story for children-- assurance of God's all encompassing love and protection.

Acknowledgements

I want to say thank you to all of the researchers, clinicians, and professors in our field whose ideas have been foundational in helping to shape the way that I understand, teach, and treat trauma. I could never begin to name each one individually, but the resources listed here are some that I highly value. I am truly thankful for each person who has helped me create this book by paving the way through their own contributions to our field. I also want to say a special thank you to the LIFT team for all of your thoughts, contributions, and prayers. Thank you to my best friend for always believing in me and to Mrs. Janet for making the story come alive. Finally, thank you to my family and most of all to Jesus for the guidance of the Holy Spirit and for all of your love, support, and relational connections, which helped this dream come to life. My prayer is that it serves as a light for others.

Resources for Parents and Caregivers

https://www.youversion.com/the-bible-app-for-kids/

https://childmind.org/guide/helping-children-cope-traumatic-event/

https://www.drdansiegel.com/books/the_whole_brain_child/

https://www.circleofsecurityinternational.com

https://www.a4pt.org

https://www.platimebox.com

https://www.acesconnection.com

About This Book

My hope, as a mother and mental health professional, is that this book may provide a model through which adults can help the children in their lives make sense of adverse experiences. When we experience an event that exceeds our current ability to understand, cope, and integrate, it can be defined as a trauma.

As the adverse or traumatic experience is absorbed by our brain, it often remains separated from the part of our brain that helps us make sense of our experiences until we have enough resources in place to help us fully digest, process, and begin to understand how the event fits into our life story.

For example, the terrible hurricane Hope processes with her grandmother in this book can be defined as trauma. While the memory of the experience is waiting to be made whole, that separated part may easily be triggered in situations where we are reminded of the danger. This happens in an effort to protect us, which can be helpful. However, it may also lead to unreasonable fears and even anxiety, panic attacks, and post traumatic stress symptoms.

There is no timeline or manual for how and when the processing should happen. Sometimes it requires the help of a specially trained professional. Sometimes it happens in the presence of an attuned caregiver.

Please prayerfully seek professional help if you become concerned about your child following an adverse experience in their lives. We are designed to heal and children are incredibly resilient. Sometimes meeting with a registered play therapist, who is trauma-informed, can be tremendously helpful.

A hard thing happened . . .

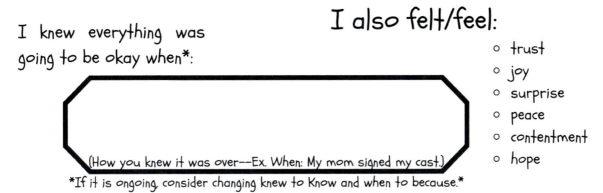

I knew everything was going to be okay when*:

(How you knew it was over--Ex. When: My mom signed my cast.)

If it is ongoing, consider changing knew to Know and when to because.

I also felt/feel:
- trust
- joy
- surprise
- peace
- contentment
- hope

Put it Away:

What your box would be made of?

What kind of lid would it have?

How would you keep it closed?

Who would you ask to hold it for you?

Asking someone we trust (like Jesus or our favorite grown up) to HOLD the scary or hard things for us can really help! It works well to imagine placing it in a container first. Then using your imagination give it to someone you TRUST--Watch them take it away and put it in a SAFE place until it is a good time to think about it again.

With a pencil draw a picture or write words that represent the scary thing. With dark colored markers color over the scary thing to close the box. Now You can Put it Away however you choose!

© Beautiful Creation 2020

www.youareabeautifulcreation.com

God gives us lots of Helpers along the way!

When I was a boy and I would see scary things in the news, my mother would say to me, "Look for the helpers. You will always find people who are helping." To this day, especially in times of "disaster," I remember my mother's words and I am always comforted by realizing that there are still so many helpers – so many caring people in this world. ~FRED ROGERS~

People   Places   Things

My Helpers:

God designed our brain and body to Help us!

We can use our five senses to help calm down and feel better when we are scared, sad, or angry. You can create your very own calm down kit just like Hope! Make a list of things you love using your five senses. Then create your kit by putting reminders from your list into a shoebox or bag.

Hear	See	Smell	Taste	Touch

Psalm 121, 139 and Isaiah 45:3

God gives us Hidden Treasures!

Treasures I have found:

© Beautiful Creation 2020
www.youareabeautifulcreation.com